P9-DDB-325

Dear Parent,

The My First Steps to Reading® *series is based on a teaching activity that helps children learn to recognize letters and their sounds. The use of predictable language patterns and repetition of familiar words will also help your child build a basic sight vocabulary. Your child will enjoy watching the characters in the books place imaginative objects in "letter boxes." You and your child can even create and fill your own letter box, using stuffed animals, cut-out pictures, or other objects beginning with the same letter. The things you can do together are limited only by your imagination. Learning letters will be fun—the first important step on the road to reading.*

The Editors

© 2001 The Child's World, Inc.
All Rights Reserved. Published by Scholastic Inc., 90 Old Sherman Turnpike, Danbury, Connecticut 06810,
by arrangement with The Child's World, Inc.
Scholastic offers a varied selection of children's book racks and tote bags. For details about ordering, please write to:
Scholastic At Home, 90 Old Sherman Turnpike, Danbury, CT 06810, Attention: Premium Department

Originally published as *My "h" Sound Box* by The Child's World, Inc.

My First Steps to Reading is a registered trademark of Grolier Publishing Co. Inc.
SCHOLASTIC and associated logos are trademarks and/or registered trademarks of Scholastic Inc.

No part of this publication may be reproduced, or stored in a retrieval system, or transmitted in any form or by any means,
electronic, mechanical, photocopying, recording, or otherwise, without written permission of the publisher.
For information regarding permission, write to The Child's World, Inc., P.O. Box 326, Chanhassen, MN 55317.
ISBN 0-7172-6507-2

Printed in the U.S.A.

My "h" Book

written by Jane Belk Moncure

illustrated by Colin King

Little  had a box.

"I will find things that begin
with my 'h' sound," he said.

"I will put them into my sound 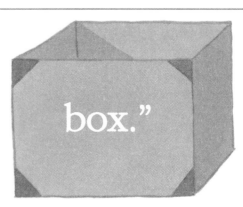 box."

He found some  hats.

He put a hat on his  head.

Did he put the other hats into his box?

He did.

Little  found a hen.

"Hello," he said. "I need a hen for my sound box." He put the hen into his box with the hats.

Then he found a hog.

Did he put the hog into his box with the hen and the hats?

He did.

Little  h found a horse.

He was happy.
He hopped onto
the horse.

He rode the horse up a high hill.

"I want to go higher," said Little .
But the horse could not go
higher. They were on top of the hill.

So Little

put the horse into
his box with the
hats, the hen, and
the hog.

Then he found a

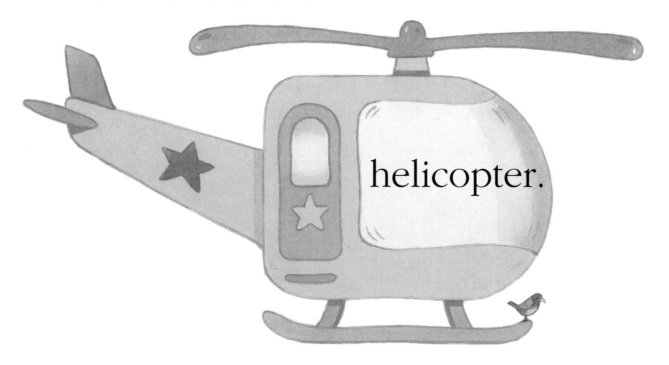

helicopter.

"Now I can go very high," he said,
"higher than a hill."

The helicopter went so high that the hen, the hog, and the horse cried, "Help! Help!"

So Little  put the helicopter into the box.

Now the box was heavy. Little
put it on his head.

He did not see the   hole.

He hopped into the hole.

"Help! Help!"

"How can we get out of this  hole?"

asked the hen,

the hog,

and the horse.

Happily, Little  h happened

to have a horn.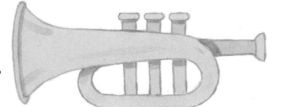

"I will blow my
horn," he said.

He blew the horn.

A 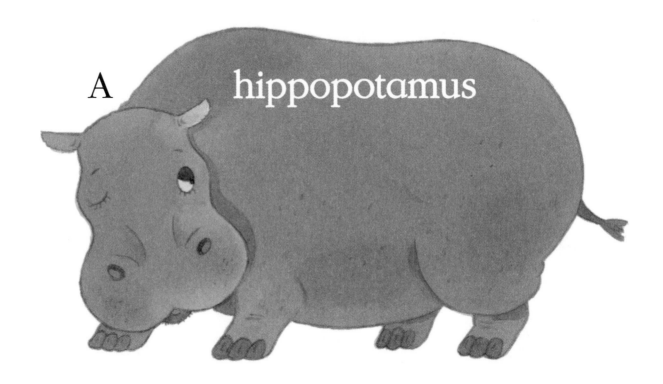 hippopotamus

heard the horn.

He helped them out of the hole.

"Hurrah for the hippo!"
everyone shouted happily.

"How can I thank you for helping
us out of the hole?"

    asked Little 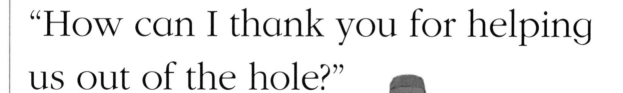 .

"You can take me for a
    ride in the helicopter,"

said the   hippopotamus.

So Little  took the helicopter out of the box.

He and all the animals went for a ride.

They flew high over a hill . . .

and all the way home.

There, Little  h spread out his things.

hen

horn

horse

helicopter

hats

hog

hippopotamus

My! How many he had!

Can you read these words
with Little  ?

hair

hot dog

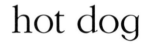

honey

harp

hand

 hummingbird

 hood

 hamburger

hammer

 hospital

 heart